Lights, Camera... Liftoff!

For Judith and Zack. The truth is out there.
—D.G.

Lights, Camera... Liftoff!

by Dan Greenburg
illustrated by Macky Pamintuan

A STEPPING STONE BOOK™

Random House New York

Copyright © 2007 by Dan Greenburg
Illustrations copyright © 2007 by Macky Pamintuan

Published in the United States by Random House Children's Books,
a division of Random House, Inc., New York.

RANDOM HOUSE and colophon are registered trademarks and
A STEPPING STONE BOOK and colophon are trademarks of
Random House, Inc.

www.steppingstonesbooks.com
www.randomhouse.com/kids

Educators and librarians, for a variety of teaching tools, visit us at
www.randomhouse.com/teachers

Library of Congress Cataloging-in-Publication Data
Greenburg, Dan.
Lights, camera . . . liftoff! / by Dan Greenburg ;
illustrated by Macky Pamintuan. — 1st ed.
p. cm. — (Weird planet ; 5)
"A Stepping Stone book."
SUMMARY: Siblings Klatu, Lek, and Ploo, along with their human friends
Lily and Jo-Jo, travel to Hollywood, California, where the aliens become
extras on a science fiction television show while waiting for the spaceship
that will take them home.
ISBN 978-0-375-84336-5 (pbk.) — ISBN 978-0-375-94336-2 (lib. bdg.)
[1. Extraterrestrial beings—Fiction. 2. Brothers and sisters—Fiction.
3. Television—Production and direction—Fiction. 4. Hollywood (Los Angeles,
Calif.)—Fiction. 5. Science fiction. 6. Humorous stories.]
I. Pamintuan, Macky, ill. II. Title.
PZ7.G8278Lig 2007
[Fic]—dc22   2006103330

Printed in the United States of America
10 9 8 7 6 5 4 3 2 1
First Edition

Contents

Your Ride Is Here—
Are You Ready?

"Ploo, you're my best nonhuman girl-friend," said Lily. "Actually, you're my *only* nonhuman girlfriend. I'm so sad you're leaving, I can't stand it."

Ploo took the hand of her new friend from Earth. Lily's skin was an ugly pinkish color, not the lovely dark gray of Looglings. Her hand had five fingers instead of the normal three. Lily also had strange yellow hair and no antenna growing out of her head. But Ploo loved her just the same.

"And you are my very best *human* friend," said Ploo. "I cannot stand it, either. But I shall come back to see you."

"Promise?" said Lily. "Cross your heart and hope to die?"

"I certainly do not hope to die," said Ploo. "But I promise."

Ploo and her two brothers had crash-landed on Earth several weeks earlier. Their spaceship was busted. But a new one was coming for them. It would touch down any minute now.

"What about me and Klatu?" asked Lek, Ploo's brother. "Are you glad that *we* are leaving?"

"Of course not, silly," said Lily. "I'm sad that all of you are leaving. I wish I could come with you."

"Oh, then why not come?" asked Klatu. "It would be so cold!"

"You mean *cool*?" said Lily.

"No, *cold*," said Klatu. "On the Darkside of Loogl, we almost never see the sun."

It was late night in the Nevada desert. The kids and their human friend Jo-Jo waited nervously in Jo-Jo's pink Cadillac. A message on Ploo's tiny looglphone had come through a few hours earlier. It said a spaceship was headed to Earth to pick them up tonight. Lily had come along to say goodbye.

They waited in silence. The heat of the day was gone. The sand was cool instead of burning hot. The sad *yip-yip-arooo* of a lonely coyote made Lek shiver.

"What was that?" he whispered.

"Just an ol' coyote," said Jo-Jo.

"Am I afraid of ol' coyotes?" whispered Lek.

"Darlin', you're afraid of everything,"

said Jo-Jo. "But that ol' coyote ain't hardly more than a puppy dog. He won't hurt you. Ploo, what time is the spaceship supposed to land?"

"Around midnight," said Ploo.

Jo-Jo glanced at her watch. "Well, it's nearly one-thirty now," she said. "I wonder what's happened to it."

"Maybe it got off the wormhole at the wrong universe," said Klatu.

"Maybe it got swallowed up by the mother ship from planet Graceland," said Lek. "Maybe the pilot is now being eaten alive by evil Elvises."

Klatu, Lek, and Ploo had defeated an invasion of alien Elvises in Las Vegas. It still made Lek nervous to think about all those sideburns and sequins.

In the black sky above them, they spotted a bright white light.

"Look, Aunt Jo-Jo!" cried Lily. "Is that the spaceship? Or is it Venus?" Venus is a planet that looks like a star in the night sky.

"Whatever it is," said Jo-Jo, "I'd say it's coming in for a landing."

The bright white light was getting closer.

"Unless Venus has small blue and green lights," said Lek, "that is the spaceship."

Lek was right. It was definitely a spaceship.

The spaceship was silver and round and flat. It looked like a large pot cover. It didn't make a sound as it came closer and closer. When it was nearly on the ground, it kicked up a huge cloud of dust and sand.

Suddenly a pair of bright headlights came bouncing over a hill.

"Oh no!" said Lily.

"It's a jeep from Area 51!" said Jo-Jo.

"We are doomed!" cried Lek.

Danger! esped Ploo to the pilot of the spaceship. She hoped he was close enough to pick up on her thoughts.

The jeep skidded to a stop a few yards away. Searchlights stabbed the night. Four guards jumped out of the jeep.

The air was filled with dust and sand. It was hard to see or breathe.

Take off now or they will capture you! Ploo esped.

With a huge burst of swirling sand, the spaceship rose straight up. Then, without a sound, it vanished into the night.

Klatu, Lek, Ploo, Lily, and Jo-Jo cheered.

"Why are we cheering?" asked Klatu. "That was the spaceship we have been waiting for. And it has just taken off without us."

"Klatu is right," said Lek. "We are *varnas* to cheer."

The four guards stared up into the dark sky. They looked upset. Then one of them walked over to the pink Cadillac. Even though it was dark out, he wore sunglasses with mirrored lenses. Klatu, Lek, and Ploo scrunched down and hid under the seats.

"What are you people doing here, ma'am?" he asked Jo-Jo.

"Just watchin' the UFO," said Jo-Jo.

"What UFO is that, ma'am?" said the guard.

"The one that almost landed and took off again," said Jo-Jo.

"That was no UFO," said the guard. "That was a weather balloon."

"Whatever you say, hon," said Jo-Jo.

"This is a secured area," said the guard. "You may not remain here."

"Oh, hogwash," said Jo-Jo. "This is the desert. We're not breakin' any laws."

"If you don't leave right away," said the guard, "I'll have to take you back to my superior officer."

"You mean Major Paine?" said Jo-Jo. "He's an old buddy of mine. I used to be a mechanic at Area 51."

Lily stayed quiet. Major Paine was her daddy. She didn't think she should mention it, though.

"Well, you aren't a mechanic there now, so move along," said the guard.

"It's because of folks like you that I quit workin' at Area 51, darlin'," said Jo-Jo.

She turned on the engine and drove away.

"That was a close one," said Lek. "If he had looked under the seats, he would have seen us."

"We have missed our ride back to planet Loogl," said Ploo.

"I'm sure it'll come back for y'all soon," said Jo-Jo.

"Maybe it'll even come back tomorrow night," said Lily.

"Maybe it will," said Lek. "And maybe it will not. But when it does, the same thing will happen. We are doomed to stay on Earth forever!"

The Gamma Wormhole

"We shall never again see our precious planet Loogl," said Lek as they drove through the desert. He stared up at the black sky, where the spaceship had disappeared. "We shall never again eat *patkas* and *karpas* at the beginning of *Snargleploom* and watch the six moons of Loogl rise over the Darkside." He sighed.

"You know, Lek may be right," said

Jo-Jo. "It might really be too dangerous for y'all to meet up with that spaceship so close to Area 51."

"Maybe another place will be safer," said Ploo.

"Maybe Las Vegas," said Lek. "No one will even notice a spaceship landing there. They thought the Elvis invasion was a stage show."

The wind started up, blowing tumbleweeds across the road. In the ghostly light of the moon, they looked like living things.

"I just got a better idea," said Jo-Jo. "A buddy of mine used to work with me at Area 51, fixin' up crashed UFOs. He's now got a job in TV—"

"In Hollyhocks?" Klatu broke in excitedly.

"It's Holly*wood*, hon, not Hollyhocks," said Jo-Jo. "Have y'all ever heard of a TV series called *Space Kids in La-La Land*? It's about three kids from outer space. They get jobs at a diner in Los Angeles."

"They have stolen our life story!" said Klatu. "We shall have to dress them in law suits!"

"No, hon," said Jo-Jo. "The show's been on TV since before y'all got here. Anyway, my friend is working on that show. He's a big-deal producer. They have lots of mockups of spaceships on the set. So if a *real* spaceship showed up one day, it might not cause too much of a fuss."

"I think it would be thrilling to go to Hollyhocks," said Klatu. "I have always wanted to be in an Earth TV show!"

Jo-Jo laughed. "Klatu, not everyone who goes to Hollywood becomes a star!"

"Maybe I can come with you," said Lily.

At first Lily's dad had been very mad when Lily went to Las Vegas with Jo-Jo. But then Lily told him all about the Elvis aliens. He took off for Vegas and forgot to even ground her.

Ploo had been very quiet. Finally she spoke up.

"I must warn you about something," said Ploo. "The Gamma Wormhole will close in seven days."

"What's the Gamma Wormhole, hon?" asked Jo-Jo.

"It is a space wormhole between Earth and planet Loogl. It allows very fast travel between galaxies," said Ploo. "So whatever happens, we must do it in the next seven days. After that, the Gamma Wormhole will close up. Then we really *will* be stuck here on Earth."

Looglings in Hollyhocks

Three days later, Jo-Jo's pink Cadillac cruised into Los Angeles. Lek, Klatu, Lily, and Ploo stared at all the strange sights. The Looglings wore big hats and sunglasses so people wouldn't notice they were aliens.

The streets were lined with palm trees. Their huge fronds swayed gently in the breeze and made nice rustling sounds. The air was warm and smelled like orange blossoms. They saw lots of sports cars on the

streets—Corvettes, MGs, and BMWs in bright reds and yellows, with their tops down. They saw lots of people on the sidewalks, with dark tans and big sunglasses. Klatu, Lek, and Ploo tried to imagine the people looking better. With bigger heads, bigger eyes, antennas, and gray skin, they might even be pretty.

"Look out!" screamed Lek.

Jo-Jo jumped. The car swerved, narrowly missing a palm tree.

A giant boy had frightened Lek. But it wasn't real. It was a big cement statue outside Bob's Big Boy drive-in. The plump boy in red-and-white-checked overalls held a hamburger on a plate above his head. He looked like a chubby Statue of Liberty.

"Darlin', that boy isn't alive," said Jo-Jo. "He's a statue."

"But he has a *shmendler* in his hand!" cried Lek.

"That's a giant hamburger," said Lily.

"And those are not dangerous?" said Lek.

"Not unless you eat too many of them," said Jo-Jo.

"Lek, you are really *vonko*," said Klatu.

Ploo and Lily looked at each other, rolled their eyes, and giggled.

Jo-Jo drove past Grauman's Chinese Theatre on Hollywood Boulevard. It looked like a big red Chinese temple. A ferocious dragon snaked across the front of the building. Tiny dragons raced down the sides of the theater's pale green copper roof. Big stone animals, half lion, half dog, guarded the main doors.

"Kids, this is the most famous movie theater on Earth," said Jo-Jo. "Let's get out and take a look."

Lek stumbled as he stepped out of the car. The sidewalks in front of Grauman's Chinese Theatre were bumpy with pressed-in handprints and footprints. Around them, names were scratched into the cement.

"How did these handprints and footprints get here?" asked Ploo.

"I read about this in my Earth Studies class," said Klatu. He gave them a knowing look. "People jumped off the roof and landed hard on the sidewalk."

"Don't be silly," said Lily. "People stuck their hands and feet in the cement before it dried."

"Did they get in trouble for doing that?" Ploo asked.

"No," said Lily. "They were movie stars."

"If they had been ordinary people, they would have been in trouble," said Lek.

"*Big* trouble," said Klatu.

Jo-Jo drove down Wilshire Boulevard to the La Brea Tar Pits. On one side of the wide street was a black lake with animal statues in it.

"Do not stop the car!" said Lek. "There is a family of elephants in that lake. They have the longest tusks I have ever seen!"

"That black lake is tar," said Jo-Jo. "Some of the best fossils on Earth have come out of it. And those elephants are woolly mammoths." Before Lek could say anything, she hurried on. "They're only statues. The real ones died out about nine thousand years ago."

"They still look pretty scary to me," said Lek. "Please do not stop."

Ploo and Lily giggled.

Jo-Jo drove them to the beach in Santa Monica. Rollerbladers zipped along the boardwalk, dodging the people who were

only walking. Huge waves thundered onto
the sand, then pulled out again with a hiss.
Spray from the breaking waves sparkled in
the sunlight. Surfers rode the big, curling
breakers into shore on their surfboards.

"Look!" Klatu shouted. "Surfin' U.S.A.!"

"Catch a wave and you're sitting on top of the world!" yelled Lek. "Do you love me, surfer girl?" he sang in a strange, high voice.

"How do you know about surfing and catching waves?" asked Jo-Jo.

"Oh, *everybody* on Loogl knows the Beach Boys songs," said Ploo.

Jo-Jo drove them back from the beach along Sunset Boulevard. Soon they entered Beverly Hills. Behind tall hedges, the kids caught quick glimpses of amazing houses. Some of them had pillars on the front and looked like temples in ancient Greece. Some had marble statues and splashing fountains. They all had huge iron gates to keep strangers out.

"I got us rooms at the Beverly Hills Hotel," said Jo-Jo. "It's a pretty fancy place. They'd probably freak out at the sight of aliens. Why don't y'all morph into human shapes?"

Looglings were able to morph into the

shape of anything they liked. The new shapes only lasted an *arp*. An *arp* of Loogl time was about the same as an hour of Earth time. After that, they would change back into alien shape.

"And pop in some new gum while you're at it," Jo-Jo added.

Looglings always traveled to other planets with special language gum balls. If they chewed up a green one, they could speak English till the flavor faded, about an *arp*. If they chewed up a red one, they could speak Spanish. There was a different color for every language.

"Okay, gang," said Klatu. "Get ready to morph. Here we go. One . . . two . . . three . . . morph!"

With a soft popping sound, Klatu, Lek, and Ploo grew outward and upward. Their heads got smaller, but their legs and arms

25

got thicker. Their eyes shrank down to beady little Earthling size.

They'd been on Earth for several weeks now. When they first came, they were morphing into clothes and haircuts they'd seen in their Earth Studies textbooks. But they'd had no idea how old their textbooks were. They'd chosen old-fashioned sailor suits with short pants, button-up shoes, and straw hats with ribbons. Now they knew better. They morphed into what they'd seen people wear in Las Vegas. Flowered shirts, shorts, and flip-flops.

"Here we are," said Jo-Jo. "The Pink Palace."

She pulled up into the long driveway of the Beverly Hills Hotel. The pink Spanish-style buildings were surrounded by tropical trees and flower beds. Pink towers with flags on top stuck out of the roofs. Tall palm trees were everywhere. In the hotel driveway, Jo-Jo's pink Cadillac didn't look at all out of place among the Jaguars, Ferraris, and Rolls-Royces.

A man in uniform came up to the car.

"Are you guests at the hotel?" he asked.

"Yes, hon," said Jo-Jo. "We're checkin' in."

"Very well, ma'am," said the man. He opened the doors. Everybody got out. The man got into the Cadillac and drove it away.

"Hey, that man just stole our car!" cried Lek. "What shall we do? Without it we are doomed!"

People turned to stare at Lek.

"He didn't steal our car, darlin'," said Jo-Jo. "He just drove it to the hotel garage."

"Oh," said Lek.

"Is that a movie star?" asked Klatu. He

pointed to a blond woman wearing big
sunglasses.

"I don't think so," said Jo-Jo.

"Are you a movie star?" Klatu asked the
woman.

The woman smiled and shook her

head. "No," she said, "but I *am* writing a screenplay."

"Oooh," said Lek. "Could we see it?"

Four days had passed since the spaceship tried to pick them up. Ploo was getting worried. In only three more days, the Gamma Wormhole would close. So first thing in the morning, Jo-Jo drove them out to the TV studio.

The studio where they filmed *Space Kids in La-La Land* was north of Hollywood. Jo-Jo's producer friend, Mickey, came out to meet them.

"Hi, guys!" said Mickey.

He had a short beard and wore sunglasses and a baseball cap. He took them to metal buildings the size of airplane hangars. Inside, the crew had built all the sets used in the show.

"Jumping *jeblonskies*!" cried Lek. "There is a whole street inside this building!"

Klatu, Lek, Ploo, Lily, and Jo-Jo were given a tour. One set looked exactly like a diner on a Los Angeles street. It was where the Space Kids worked. Just outside the diner, they had built a sidewalk with a fake mailbox, fake parking meters, and a fake fire hydrant.

Inside the diner, there were booths and a counter with stools. On the counter were cakes and pies with whipped cream on top. Klatu took a bite out of one. "Yum!" he said.

Jo-Jo laughed. "That isn't real cake, hon," she said. "That's a prop."

"What is a prop?" asked Klatu.

"Props are things the actors use in the show," said Jo-Jo. "That one is fake cake. It's made out of Styrofoam."

"I like fake cake," said Klatu. "I also like

Styrofoam. It tastes even better than wood or paper."

Another set looked like the Hollywood apartment where the Space Kids lived. It had beds, chairs, couches, a tiny kitchen, and a bathroom. Right next to it was a set that looked like the apartment where some of the Space Kids' human friends lived.

High above the sets, instead of a ceiling, were hundreds of spotlights and miles of wiring. There were also many microphones. Two huge cameras on carts with rubber wheels stood at the edge of the sets.

"It is nice that the Space Kids can actually live here," said Lek.

"Oh, they don't live here, darlin'," said Jo-Jo. "They couldn't if they wanted to."

"Why not?"

"Because it looks like a real apartment, but it isn't," she said. "The refrigerator isn't a real refrigerator. The TVs and the radios aren't real. The faucets in the sink and the shower don't have running water in them. Nothing you see here is real."

"Nothing?" said Klatu.

"That's right."

"But the toilet in that set works, right?" said Klatu.

"Well, no, hon," said Jo-Jo. "There's no water in it and it doesn't flush."

"Uh-oh," said Klatu.

4

Half-Baked Plans

"Are you kids hungry?" Jo-Jo's friend Mickey asked after the tour. Klatu nodded quickly. Mickey led them to a big table full of food, the place where the actors and crew ate their meals. Klatu, Lek, and Ploo were still in their human shapes.

It was a warm day. Klatu took a Good Humor bar from a freezer next to the table. He unwrapped it. Then he ate the paper and the stick and threw away the ice cream.

Meanwhile, Jo-Jo was whispering with Mickey. "Can you set up an outdoor scene with a landing spaceship in three days?" she asked him. "When the spaceship lands, Klatu, Lek, and Ploo will sneak on board. The pilot can take off with them whenever he likes."

Jo-Jo and Mickey walked off together to make the plans. Lily waited till Jo-Jo was out of sight. Then she made an announcement.

"When that spaceship comes to pick you up," she said, "I'm going to sneak onto it with you."

"I think it is a fine idea," said Klatu. "I will use you for extra credit in my report for science class."

"Why do *you* get to use her?" asked Lek. "She's *my* friend, too!"

Ploo was not as sure as Klatu and Lek. Maybe it wasn't such a fine idea.

"I think that Jo-Jo will go *chimp* when she finds out," Ploo told Lily.

"You mean *ape*?" said Lily.

"Oh yes, *ape* is what I meant," said Ploo.

"Well, then, we'll just have to keep it a secret," said Lily.

"I guess so," said Ploo. Something was

bothering her, though. "Lily, I am not so sure that coming back to Loogl with us is such a good idea," she said.

"You don't want me to come with you?" Lily asked.

"I do," said Ploo. "But what about your parents? Won't they worry about you? And won't you miss them terribly? I miss *mine* terribly."

"If you don't want me to come and visit your planet," said Lily, "then why don't you just say so?" Her lower lip stuck out. She seemed hurt.

"I *do* want you to come visit us," said Ploo. "Having you there would be lovely, but . . ."

"Then it's settled," said Lily. "I'm coming." She crossed her arms.

"Okay," said Ploo.

"Uh-oh," said Lek.

"What is it?" asked Lily.

"I just had a stretchy feeling in my head," whispered Lek. He looked at the *arp*-timer on his wrist. "The *arp* is up. I am starting to morph back."

"I felt a tingle, too," said Ploo. "We can't let any humans see us like this. We had better hide."

"I do not feel a thing yet," said Klatu. "Just a little itch in my head where I . . . *Oopah!*" An antenna poked through Klatu's head.

Klatu, Lek, and Ploo ran around the corner of the diner set. They crouched down behind a booth. Their morphing was happening very quickly now. Their heads and eyes grew larger. Their arms and legs grew smaller. Their skin tone went from pink to gray.

Just then, a man with a clipboard came

around the corner and nearly stepped on them. It was a tense moment. Nobody said anything.

"Oh, hello," said the man with the clipboard. He didn't seem very surprised.

"Hello," said Klatu.

"You folks here for the auditions?" said the man.

"The what?" said Klatu.

"The auditions," said the man. "For the aliens."

Klatu, Lek, Ploo, and Lily looked at each other.

"Yes!" said Lily.

"Well, go right through that door there," he said. He pointed to a door marked CASTING.

"Okay," said Klatu.

The man walked away.

"What are *additions*?" whispered Klatu.

"*Auditions,*" whispered Lily. "It's when actors try out for parts in a movie or TV show."

"I have always wanted to be in a TV show!" said Klatu. He ran toward the door marked CASTING. Lily, Ploo, and Lek had no choice except to follow him.

"You here for the auditions?" asked a

man wearing a baseball cap. He carried a clipboard and had a whistle around his neck.

"Yes," said Ploo.

"Well, you're shorter than our usual aliens," said the man. "But we have to shoot this scene right away. So you'll have to do. Go right into Makeup. Right through that door there."

Klatu, Lek, Ploo, and Lily opened the door with the word MAKEUP on it. They thought everything was cool. They had no idea that other eyes had watched them morph. One of the show's stars, a girl named Heather, stood behind a wind machine. She tried to make sense of what she'd seen.

"Am I going nuts?" Heather said to herself. "Or did three of those kids turn into real aliens? No, that isn't possible.

Everybody knows this show is only make-believe. Everybody knows there's no such thing as real aliens or UFOs. But what if there are? What if these kids are real evil visitors from outer space? If I turn them in to the police, I could save the people of Earth! I could be a huge hero! And just think what great publicity that would be for our show! I'd better keep my eye on them till I'm sure!"

5

Remember, You're Just Actors

The makeup room smelled like hair spray. A lady in a blue smock sat in what looked like a dentist's chair, reading a magazine. She looked up as Klatu, Lek, Ploo, and Lily walked in.

"You three don't look bad," the makeup lady said to Klatu, Lek, and Ploo. She gave Ploo's antenna a flick with her fingernail. "But I can make it look better. Because, frankly, you don't look like *real* aliens."

"But we *are*," said Ploo.

The makeup lady laughed. "You guys are a little *too* into your roles," she said. "Try to remember you're just actors, okay?"

Ploo looked at Klatu and Lek. They shrugged.

"Okay," Ploo agreed.

"All right," said the makeup lady. "I'll just add some stuff to what you've already got on."

When the makeup lady had finished, Klatu, Lek, and Ploo all had spotted green skin and fangs growing out of their faces.

"Now you look like real aliens," said the makeup lady.

"You're the expert," said Klatu.

Klatu, Lek, Ploo, and Lily walked out of Makeup.

Heather was watching from behind a

fake mailbox. "Aha!" she said to herself. "Now they've made themselves up to look like fake aliens in the show. Only I know who they really are!"

"There you are!" someone shouted.

Klatu, Lek, and Ploo were standing outside in the hot sun. Their gray Looglish skin was baking under their silly alien makeup. "You're in the background of a scene that's going to be shot next," said the assistant director.

A few human extras wearing the same silly alien makeup were standing around, too. The stars of the show who played the Space Kids—Heather, Brad, and Tiffany— were standing near a mock-up of a spaceship, talking.

"See those extras over there?" whispered Heather.

Brad and Tiffany turned to look.

"So?" said Brad.

"They may be real aliens," said Heather.

"Yeah, right," said Brad. "Just like us."

"No, I'm serious," said Heather. "I actually saw them change from human shape into the way they look now!"

"I've seen that, too," said Tiffany. "It's an interesting process. It's called Wardrobe and Makeup."

"No, you guys, I mean it," Heather said. "I watched it happen right in front of my eyes. It took about thirty seconds. What if they're evil aliens from outer space? What if they're plotting to invade Earth or something?"

Brad and Tiffany giggled. "What if they are?" said Brad.

"Well, we could report them to the police," said Heather. "They'd know what to do. We could save the people of Earth and become huge heroes."

"Yeah, Heather, you do that," said Tiffany.

A man with a notepad and a camera with a telephoto lens came closer to them.

"Excuse me," said the man. "I'm Dick Fester from the *World News Report*. We're the top-selling newspaper in supermarkets all over the world. I couldn't help overhearing

you. Did you say those kids over there are real aliens and that they're plotting to invade Earth?"

"Uh, we don't exactly have any proof of that yet," said Heather.

"Oh, the *World News Report* doesn't care too much about *proof*," said Dick Fester.

He raised his camera and fired off several shots of Klatu, Lek, and Ploo with his telephoto lens.

6

What If Everyone Thinks You're Ugly?

The next morning, Klatu, Lek, Ploo, and Lily were watching the crew get ready to shoot a close-up of Heather. Heather was going to be pretending to cook hamburgers on the set that looked like the diner's kitchen. On a film set, the electricians are called gaffers. They were standing on ladders, adjusting big movie lights above Heather's head.

Actually, it wasn't Heather. It was Heather's stand-in. A stand-in is a person who stands where one of the stars is going to stand when the scene is shot. It takes a long time to light a scene and the lights are very hot. So a stand-in saves the actor from being hot and bored while the lights are being set up.

"Lily," said Ploo, "I am worried about your plan to—"

"Shhh!" said Lily, looking around.

"Jo-Jo can't hear us," said Ploo in a quiet voice. She looked at Heather's stand-in. "Nobody can hear us, not even her."

"What are you worried about?" said Lily.

"Many things," said Ploo. "I worry that you will get homesick for your family. For your friends. For your own planet. I worry that if you do, you will not be able to come back to Earth easily. I worry that—"

"Ploo, I won't get homesick, okay?" said Lily. "I've been away from my parents with you guys in Las Vegas. I'm away with you now in Los Angeles."

"But you will be the only Earthling on the whole planet," said Ploo. "What if everyone thinks you're . . . ugly?"

"I'm *not* ugly," said Lily. She tossed her curly blond hair. "Do *you* think I'm ugly?"

"Well, no," said Ploo. "Not *ugly,* really. . . ." How could she tell her friend what she truly thought without hurting her feelings? How could she say that human heads were much too small? That human eyes were tiny and beady? That Looglings were far more graceful and delicate?

"Lily," said Ploo, "could you talk it over with Jo-Jo? If Jo-Jo thinks it is a good idea, then I will not worry."

"You want me to talk this over with *Jo-Jo?*" said Lily. "Ploo, Jo-Jo is a *grown-up.* Of *course* she'd think this is a stupid idea. Grown-ups think all kids' ideas are stupid. Jo-Jo wouldn't let me go to another planet.

And she'd probably have some stupid grown-up reason. Promise me you won't tell Jo-Jo. Promise me you won't. Do you promise?"

"Well . . ."

"If you rat me out to Jo-Jo, you aren't really my friend," said Lily.

"What can I not do to Jo-Jo with a rat?" Ploo asked.

"Rat me *out*," said Lily. "It means telling Jo-Jo what I'm planning to do. If you do, you can't be my friend."

REAL ALIENS ON SPACE KIDS SET! THEY ARE PLOTTING ATTACK ON EARTH!

The headlines marched across the front page of the *World News Report*. Below was a huge picture of Klatu, Lek, and Ploo in alien form. Underneath the picture it read:

"Have you seen us? We're not on any milk carton, but we are living among you. Watching.

Waiting. Plotting to take over your planet!"

All right, that's not what the kids in the photo actually said, but they might as well have. Posing as extras in the hit TV show Space Kids in La-La Land, *the creatures pictured above are actually real aliens. They are posing as actors who are* pretending to be *aliens. Meanwhile, they are planning an invasion of Earth. . . .*

"Oh no!" Ploo put down the newspaper. "What are we going to do?" she asked.

Ploo, Lek, and Klatu were huddled together at one end of the *Space Kids* set.

"They will come after us with torches!" said Lek. "A whole village of them. I have seen it happen before in the movies."

Then a hand clamped down on Klatu's shoulder. "Aaah!" he screamed.

A man and a woman in tank tops and shorts were standing next to them.

"We just saw you guys in the paper,"

said the man. "Can we have your autographs?" He held out a pen and a copy of
the *World News Report*. "Just write them
across your picture there."

Klatu scribbled something on the picture
and handed it back.

"I can't make this out," said the woman.
She squinted at Klatu's signature. "What's
your name?"

"Klatu," said Klatu. "I wrote it in
Looglish."

I'm Not a Real Alien, but I Play One on TV

"Well, Ploo, it's all set," said Jo-Jo.

Ploo and Jo-Jo were sitting in the Polo Lounge in the hotel. The Looglings had the afternoon off. Their characters weren't needed in any scenes. Ploo and Jo-Jo were having a glass of iced tea. Lily, Lek, and Klatu were at the pool. Ploo had remained in her Looglish shape. Why not? It was already in the papers, anyway.

Ploo was taking ice cubes out of her glass

and trying to decide if she liked placing them on her skin. She liked the cold feeling, but she didn't understand why they were getting smaller and turning into water.

"My friend Mickey says we're shootin' the spaceship-landing scene tomorrow," said Jo-Jo. "The director thinks the spaceship is a special effect that Mickey set up. But it'll be your guy from Loogl, of course. Can you tell the spaceship to land here at two o'clock?"

"Two o'clock," said Ploo. "I will send a message to the pilot on the looglphone."

A woman in a black business suit came up to Jo-Jo and Ploo's table.

"Excuse me," said the woman, looking at Ploo. "Aren't you one of the actors on *Space Kids in La-La Land*? I just saw you in the papers."

"Yes," said Ploo. She was getting used

to the attention. Since this morning, three people had asked for her autograph.

"I'd love to invite you and your friends to an opening tonight," said the woman.

"What is going to open?" said Ploo. "A door? A window?"

The woman laughed. "It's a movie opening, of course. Would you like to come as our guests of honor?"

Ploo looked at Jo-Jo. Jo-Jo shrugged.

"Thank you," said Ploo. "We would love to come."

"Good," said the woman. She gave Ploo a handful of fancy invitations. "I'll send a limo to pick you up here at seven o'clock."

"Is this limo thing strong enough to pick up all five of us?" Ploo asked.

The woman laughed again. "See you at seven o'clock," she said.

Three hotel guests, all teenage girls,

came up to Jo-Jo and Ploo's table. "Aren't you one of the space aliens?" asked a girl with blond dreadlocks.

"Well, I play one on the show," said Ploo.

All three girls squealed with excitement. "I *told* you!" said the one with blond dreadlocks.

None of them said anything else to Ploo. They just snapped flash pictures of her with their cameras and held out their autograph books for her to sign.

When the limousine pulled up in front of Grauman's Chinese Theatre, it was dark out. Another limo was already at the curb ahead of them. A huge crowd of people had gathered. Searchlights carved the evening sky. A long red carpet ran from the curb to the doors of the theater. There were reporters

from several TV channels with their camera crews. There were lots of photographers.

The driver of the first limo opened the curbside door. Out climbed the stars of *Space Kids in La-La Land*—Heather, Brad, and Tiffany. Reporters, camera crews, photographers, and fans crowded around them.

Inside the second limo, Klatu, Lek,

Ploo, and Lily pressed their noses against the windows. They couldn't believe what they were seeing.

Jo-Jo took out four pairs of sunglasses and gave one to each of them. "All celebrities wear sunglasses," she said. "Put these on."

Their limo driver opened the door for

the kids. Klatu, Lek, and Ploo got out of the limo.

"What are all those people doing out there?" Klatu asked.

"They've come to see celebrities like y'all arrive for the opening," said Jo-Jo.

"What makes us celebrities?" Ploo asked.

"Y'all were on the front page of the *World News Report,* hon," said Jo-Jo. "That makes y'all celebrities."

"I am afraid," said Lek. "I fear they will attack us."

"They won't hurt you, hon," said Jo-Jo. "They just want to take your pictures and get your autographs. Go along now."

As soon as they stood on the red carpet, reporters, fans, and photographers ran over to them. The Space Kids were left alone.

"Is it true you're planning to attack planet Earth?" asked a female reporter.

"No," said Ploo. "We *love* planet Earth."

"What do you love about it?" asked a male reporter from NBC.

"We love that you can write your name in fresh cement and not get into trouble," said Lek.

"What planet are you from?" asked a female reporter from CNN.

"Planet Hollywood," said Klatu.

Everybody laughed. It was hard to tell if

the reporters really thought the kids were aliens. The photographers pressed forward. They began shooting pictures very close to the kids' faces. Even through their sunglasses, the flashes hurt their eyes. It was annoying. The kids tried to get away, but they couldn't. Everywhere they turned, more and more camera flashes popped in their faces.

Is this what it is like to be a celebrity? Ploo esped. *I do not care for it.*

Heather, Brad, and Tiffany watched all this from a few yards away.

"Those stupid kids are getting more attention than *we* are," Heather said. "And we're the *stars* of *Space Kids*. What's up with that?"

"You don't really think they're from another planet, do you?" Brad asked.

"The more I see them, the more I do,"

said Heather. She took out her cell phone and dialed 911.

"L.A. Police," said an operator. "What is your emergency?"

"There are creatures from another planet on Hollywood Boulevard," said Heather. "Outside Grauman's Chinese Theatre."

"That sounds about right," said the operator.

"You're not going to do anything about it?" Heather asked.

"Unless they're breaking any laws, it's not a police matter," said the operator.

"They're planning to attack Earth," said Heather. "Isn't *that* against the law?"

"No," said the operator. "But if you like, you could try the FBI or the army base at Area 51. Do you want those numbers?"

"Yes!" said Heather.

8

Please Hang Up and Dial Somebody Real

Lek, Ploo, and Lily were tired. They had stayed out late the night before at the movie opening. They didn't think it was a very good movie. Klatu had fallen asleep in the middle. He was the only one who wasn't tired.

The big day was finally here. The day of the spaceship landing. It was nearly two o'clock, the time that Ploo had told the ship to come. The cast and crew stood in the middle of the field, where it was going to land. The director was seated behind a large movie camera. He wore sunglasses and a Los Angeles Dodgers baseball cap. The sun was hot on everybody's skin.

Ploo, Lek, and Klatu were watching from the side. Jo-Jo and Lily were standing with them. A crowd of reporters and photographers stood in back of a fence several yards away. A dozen security people in uniform were keeping them away from Ploo, Lek, and Klatu. Everyone was waiting for the arrival of the spaceship.

Lily hated the way she'd been feeling. She hated acting like a hurt little baby around Ploo, but she couldn't help it. Ploo didn't seem to care if Lily came back to Loogl with her. Lily was ashamed of herself, but she couldn't seem to stop. If Ploo really *were* her best friend, then she'd want Lily to come. And if Ploo *wasn't* her best friend, if Ploo didn't care about her at all anymore . . .

"Jo-Jo, can I borrow your cell phone?" Lily asked.

"Sure," said Jo-Jo. She handed Lily her phone.

Lily dialed a number and waited.

"Oh, hi, Marisa," said Lily into the phone. "It's me, Lily. I'm in Hollywood. Yeah, it's a blast. How long? I don't know. Jo-Jo, how long are we going to be in Hollywood?"

"Probably just till tomorrow," said Jo-Jo. "Why?"

"Probably just till tomorrow," said Lily into the phone. "Why? Oh, really? A sleepover at your house? When? Uh-huh. How many girls will be there? Wow. Well, I don't know. I *did* have plans to go somewhere else, but your sleepover sounds really cool." Lily looked over at Ploo. "It sounds *way* more fun than what *I* was planning. I'll let you know, Marisa, okay? Bye."

This is weird, thought Ploo. *Lily talked*

on the phone, but I know there was nobody on the other end. Why would she pretend to talk with someone who was not there?

Heather, Brad, and Tiffany stood a few yards away. Heather saw Lily talking on her cell phone. She took out her own cell phone and dialed a number the 911 operator had given her. She had wanted to call the night before. But security guards had made her turn off her phone in the movie theater.

"Area 51 top-secret army base," said an operator. "How may I direct your call?"

"I want to report aliens from outer space. They are planning to attack planet Earth," said Heather in a quiet voice.

"I'll connect you with that department," said the operator.

There was a loud buzzing sound. Then: "Major Paine's office," said a gruff male voice. "Can I help you?"

"Yes," said Heather. "I want to report aliens planning an invasion of Earth."

"Are they the evil Elvises?" the voice asked eagerly.

Heather was confused. "No," she said. "They are little gray aliens. They have big, ugly heads and ugly black eyes."

"Hold on!" said the voice. "I need to grab a pencil. Then tell me everything you know!"

Nearby, Ploo turned a paler shade of gray. She had very good hearing. She had heard every word that Heather said. She had even heard what the man on the other end had said.

What if Heather got the Area 51 people out to Hollywood? They might try to capture her and her brothers. She couldn't take the chance.

Ploo closed her eyes and relaxed. She let

her antenna, thin as a straw, slide quietly out of her head. She tried to enter Heather's mind.

Heather was thinking: *I'm so jealous of those stupid alien kids. Especially that little girl with her ugly gray skin, her huge head, and her giant black eyes. If I can't get rid of them, they might even try to take away our jobs.*

Hmm.

Ploo's mind gently grasped Heather's like a lump of clay. She patted it and poked it and rolled it around. She pinched a little here, squeezed a little there. She added a few thoughts of her own and mooshed them together:

. . . I'm not really that jealous of those kids. I don't even know if they can act. Brad, Tiffany, and I are pretty good in our roles. Those kids couldn't ever really replace us. . . .

Not too bad. Ploo trickled a few more thoughts into Heather's mind:

. . . I like that little girl so much. She's so beautiful. She has such lovely black eyes and such velvety soft gray skin. It would be a shame if the Area 51 people came here and took her away. . . .

Better, much better.

"Okay, I'm ready," said the tough-sounding male voice on the other end of Heather's phone. "Please give me an exact location for the aliens you're reporting."

"Oh," said Heather. "Well, this is pretty silly. While waiting, I realized they might not be aliens at all. I mean, aliens are pretty ugly, right? And these kids are really quite beautiful."

"Wait!" the voice yelled. "Don't hang up the—"

9

All Aboard for Planet Loogl

The director raised his bullhorn to his mouth.

"All right, everybody," he called. "In a few minutes, our spaceship will be landing. Extras, when you see it, forget it was made by our producer and his friend in a garage. I want you to act as though it's a real spaceship from another planet."

High above them in the sky, a tiny silver ball appeared. It glittered in the sun.

It was almost too bright to look at directly.

"Okay, there it is," called the director. "Quiet on the set!"

The assistant director held a little blackboard with the scene number up to the camera.

"Scene fifty-four, take one," he said. "Roll sound!"

"Rolling!" called the soundman. "Speed!"

"And . . . action!" called the director.

The tiny silver ball grew larger and larger. Now it looked more like a silver saucer than a silver ball. It didn't make a sound.

In a flash, it was directly overhead.

With a swirling blast of air and dust, the spaceship slowly settled to the ground.

"Cut!" called the director. "Print that! Wow, how did you make that spaceship, Mickey?" he called to the producer. "It looks great—just like the real thing!"

"I *thought* you'd like it, Steven," said Mickey. He winked at Jo-Jo. "Wait till you see our pilot."

A panel in the silver spaceship slid open, and a Loogling stepped onto the ground.

Uh-oh, **esped Ploo.** The pilot was not supposed to get out of the spaceship!

Hey! I know that guy, **esped Klatu.** He is a kid who works at the spaceport. His name is Bork. He loves Hollyhocks movies and TV shows. He has always wanted to meet the humans who make them.

The pilot wore a space suit made out of thin, stretchy silver material. When he took off his helmet, everyone applauded. The pilot had a normal Loogling's large head, huge black eyes, and dark gray skin.

"I *love* him!" said the director. "Mickey, you didn't have to put him in Wardrobe and Makeup. He's not going to be on camera. But it's a nice touch—thanks!"

If the director talks to him, he will know Bork is an alien! esped Lek. *What can we do? We are doomed!*

Do not worry, esped Klatu. *Nobody will want to talk to Bork. He is a <u>varna</u>.*

The director got out of his seat behind the camera. He walked over to where Bork was standing.

"Nice landing," said the director. He stuck out his hand. Bork seemed puzzled. He took the director's hand in both of his. Then he raised it to his mouth.

People laughed. The director pulled his hand away.

"We're going to do another take," said the director. "The camera was a little out of focus. Can you take that thing up and land it again?"

Bork stared at the director without moving.

Quick! Does anyone have any language gum? esped Ploo.

I have some, esped Klatu.

Klatu rushed over to Bork. He handed him a language gum ball. Through ESP he told Bork to chew it up.

"What are you doing?" the director asked Klatu.

"I gave him gum," said Klatu. "Sometimes flying spaceships makes your mouth so dry, you cannot talk."

"Oh, right," said the director.

Bork chewed up the gum ball.

"*Hola, señor,*" said Bork. "*Tengo dos hermanas. Mi padre es guardia. Quiero ser médico. ¿Dónde está el baño?*"

"Huh?" said the director.

"Jo-Jo, what did he say?" whispered Lily.

"Well," whispered Jo-Jo, "he said hello, he has two sisters, his father is a police-·man, he'd like to be a doctor, and where are the toilets?"

Klatu, you varna, esped Lek, *that is Spanish! Did you give him a red gum ball instead of a green one?*

Sorry, esped Klatu. He held his hand under Bork's mouth and made spitting sounds.

Bork spit the red gum ball into Klatu's hand. He also spit a lot of saliva into it. Klatu wiped his hand off. Then he popped a green gum ball into Bork's mouth. Bork chewed it up.

"Hello, sir," said Bork. "I am honored to meet a real filmmaker."

"Um, thanks," said the director. "As I was saying, we're going to do another take on the landing. Can you get that thing up in the air and do it again?"

"Yes, sir," said Bork.

"Great," said the director.

He went back to his seat behind the

camera. Bork climbed back into the spaceship. He left the sliding panel open.

Why did he leave the panel open? esped Lek.

That is what he has been told to do, esped Ploo. *So that we could quickly climb aboard just before he took off. We'll close it once we're above the clouds.*

Does Lily still want to go to Loogl? esped Klatu.

That is not clear, esped Ploo.

"Okay," called the director through his bullhorn. "We're going for a second take. Quiet on the set!"

Lily had been wrestling with her problem for hours. Should she sneak on board the spaceship and go to Loogl with Ploo, Lek, and Klatu? Or would it be too weird and lonely on another planet?

At last she knew what she would do. She wasn't going to sneak onto the spaceship after all. In fact, she wasn't even going to watch it take off. She couldn't bear to watch her friends get on board. She couldn't bear knowing that she would never see them again.

Lily turned her back to the spaceship. She faced the film crew instead.

The assistant director held his little blackboard up to the camera for the second time.

"Scene fifty-four, take two," he said. "Roll sound!"

"Rolling!" called the soundman. "Speed!"

"And . . . action!" called the director. "Cue the pilot!"

The spaceship let out a blast of air that blew sand and dust in all directions. Then it rose straight up into the air. When it was high overhead, Lily looked up and watched it grow smaller and smaller in the distance. She felt sad enough to cry. But she wasn't a baby. She knew that she had made the right choice.

"And . . . cut!" called the director. "Okay, I don't think that panel on the spaceship should have been open. Let's do a third take. Can you call the pilot back?"

"I don't think so, Steven," said Mickey. Then he turned to somebody Lily couldn't see. "Can we call the pilot back?" he asked.

"No," said a familiar voice. "By now he is at least a galaxy away."

Lily froze. Could it possibly be who she thought it was? *Ploo?*

She turned around. It *was* Ploo! And Lek and Klatu were standing right beside her!

"Ploo!" screamed Lily. "I can't *believe* this! You didn't go?"

"No," said Ploo, "we did not."

"We decided to stay here awhile," said Lek.

"But I thought you missed your parents," said Lily.

"I do miss them," said Ploo. "We will try to return to Loogl when the next window opens up in the Gamma Wormhole. In the meantime, we will be stars of human television—if we can get rid of the photographers."

"Ploo," said Lily, "I have to tell you something stupid."

"What?"

"There never was a sleepover," said Lily. "There never was a Marisa. I made the whole thing up."

"I know," said Ploo.

"Why didn't you go back to Loogl?" Lily asked.

"I could not," said Ploo. "You are my best friend, Lily. I could not stand to leave you."

Ploo reached out her skinny gray Looglish arms. Lily walked into them and hugged her friend. Both of them had tears in their eyes. They had never been happier.

Klatu, Lek, and Ploo are off on a wild ride!
Don't miss the sixth exciting book in
the weird planet series.

weird planet 6

Thrills, Spills,
and Cosmic Chills

by Dan Greenburg
illustrated by Macky Pamintuan